MARTIN AUER

THE BLUE BOY

illustrated by

SIMONE KLAGES

LONDON
GOLLANCZ CHILDREN'S PAPERBACKS
1992

Originally published in West Germany 1991
by Beltz Verlag
under the title *Der blaue Junge*

First published in Great Britain 1992
by Victor Gollancz Ltd
14 Henrietta Street, London WC2E 8QJ

Published in Gollancz Children's Paperbacks 1992

A catalogue record for this book is
available from the British Library

ISBN 0 575 05302 X

Printed and bound in Hong Kong by Imago Publishing Ltd

Far away
beyond the stars
lies a strange galaxy.

And deeper in space
beyond swirling planets,
the universe is stranger still.

But if you travelled even further into space,
almost as far as you could go, you might eventually
reach a planet that is quite like our own.

On this distant world
which is about as big as our earth,
live people who look just like us,
except that they are blue
and have ears that they can shut tight
when they don't want to listen.

Once, a terrible war
broke out on the planet,
and many of the blue people were killed.

Most of the
children were left
orphaned, and a blue boy sat
in the ruins of his home and wept,
because his
mother and
father had died.

He cried and cried,

until he had
no tears left,
then he stood up,

turned up the collar of his jacket,
stuck his hands in his pockets and walked away.

When he saw a stone,
he kicked it,

and when he saw a flower,
he trod on it.

A little dog came up to him,
stared at him and wagged its tail.

It turned around and
began to follow him.

"Go away!"
said the boy.

"If you come with me
I shall have to look after you,
and I never want to care about anyone, ever again."

The dog looked at him
and wagged its tail cheerfully.

Then the boy picked up a gun
that lay beside a dead soldier.

He held it up and showed it to the dog.
"I could kill you with this gun!"
he said angrily.

The dog ran away.

"You may come with me,"
said the boy to the gun.
"You'll be a true friend."

And he fired
the gun
at a dead tree.

He found an abandoned plane.

He climbed inside
and tried
the ignition.

The plane took off.

"Now I've got a gun and a plane,"
said the boy.
"They'll be my family.
I could have kept the dog,
but if someone had killed it,
I'd have died of a broken heart, too."

He flew along
until he noticed a house.

"Someone still lives there," the boy said.

He flew around the house
and looked through the window.

There was an old woman,
preparing a meal.

The boy landed his plane,
loaded his gun and went inside.

"I've got a gun,"
said the boy to the old woman.

"Give me something to eat!"

"I would have given you something anyway," said the old woman. "Put away your gun."

"Don't give me any of your kindness!" said the boy. "I could shoot you if I wanted to."

So the old woman gave him some food,

and he flew on.

That was how he lived.

He made himself a den
in a deserted house.

When he was hungry
he flew to wherever
people lived,

and with his gun, forced them
to give him something to eat.

Then he would fly over the deserted battlefields
collecting the bits of junk
that were lying there.

He brought them all back to his den.

"I'll build myself a mighty robot tank,"
he said.

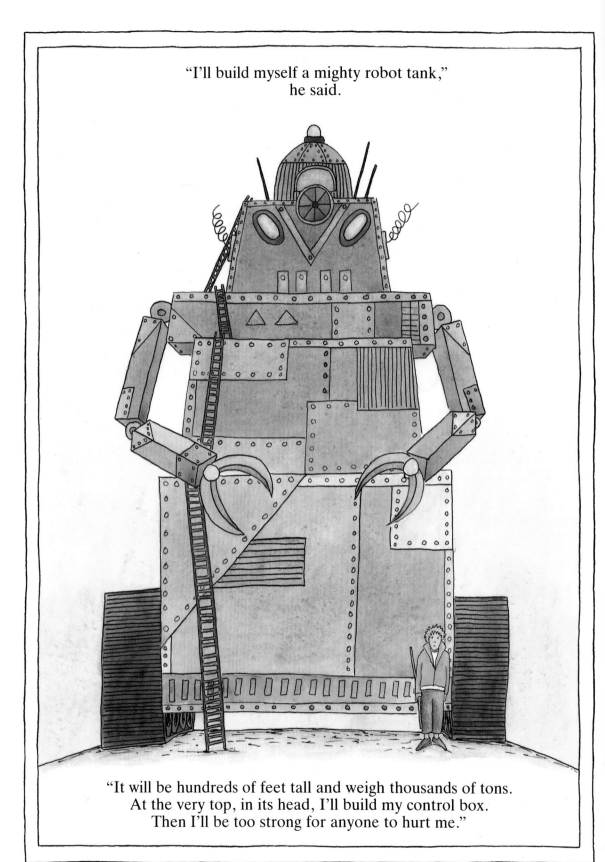

"It will be hundreds of feet tall and weigh thousands of tons.
At the very top, in its head, I'll build my control box.
Then I'll be too strong for anyone to hurt me."

One day, a girl came past
the boy's den.

He picked up his gun, went outside and said,
"Go away or I'll shoot you!"

"I won't hurt you,"
said the girl.
"I was just looking to see if the mushrooms were growing again."

"You must go away!"
said the boy.
"I won't have anyone near me."

"Are you all alone?"
asked the girl.

"No," replied the boy. "I've got a gun and a plane.
That's my family."

"And one day I'll also
have a mighty
robot tank!"

"But have you
no real friends?"
asked the girl.

"I could have had a dog.
But if anyone had killed it, I'd have died of sadness too."

"No one cares about me,"
said the girl.
"We could look after each other."

"I don't want friends
who might be killed."

"Oh!" said the girl.
"How can you find someone who
can't be killed?"

and she went on.

The boy built

his mighty
robot tank

and climbed inside.

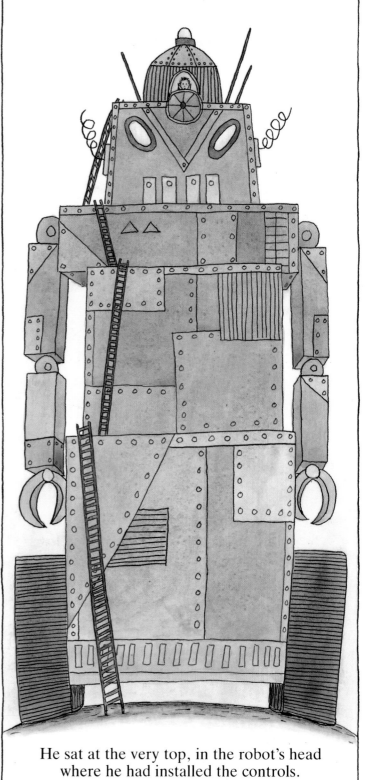

He sat at the very top, in the robot's head
where he had installed the controls.

Then he set off,
patrolling the country in his robot tank.

Whenever people saw him coming
they tried to run away,
but there was no escaping the mighty robot tank.

High in the robot's head
the boy had
a microphone.

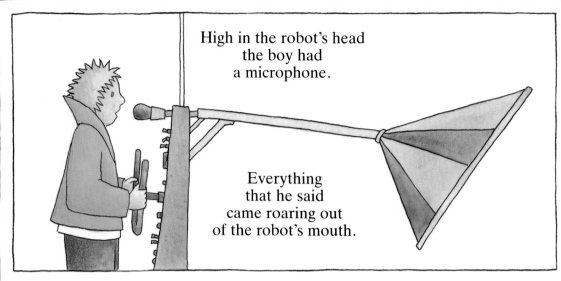

Everything
that he said
came roaring out
of the robot's mouth.

"Are any of you safe from bombs and bullets?"
roared the robot tank.

But wherever he went, the people ran away
and he never found anyone who couldn't be killed.

Then one day, he looked down
and saw that someone below
was still standing there, shouting up at him.

But he was much too high to hear.

Maybe that's the
person I've been
looking for, thought
the boy, and he
clambered down.

It was only the old woman
who had once given him food.

"Do you want to tell me something?" asked the boy.

"Yes," said the old woman.
"I've heard about a man who is safe from all our weapons.
I thought you should know about him."

"And who's that?"
asked the boy.

"He's an old man
who lives on the moon."

"Then I must try and find him,"
said the boy. "Maybe he will be my friend."

And he pulled a lever,
and his tank turned into a rocket ship and
carried him to the moon.

On the moon the boy searched high and low.

At last
he found the old
man sitting beside a
telescope, gazing down at the blue planet.

"Are you the one that nobody can kill?"
asked the boy.
"I think so," said the old man.

"What are you looking at?"
"I'm studying the people down there."

"May I stay here with you?" asked the boy.
"Perhaps," said the old man.
"But why would you want to stay with me?"

"Because I want to be with someone
who can't be hurt by bombs and bullets.
When my parents died,
I cried until I had no tears left.
I could have had a dog,
but it would have killed me
if anything had happened to it.
I could have been close to an old woman,
or a girl I met,
but they had no protection either,
and if anything had happened to them,
I'd have died of sadness too."

"Very well," said the old man. "You may stay with me. I am safe because there are no weapons here."

"Is that the reason?" "Yes, that's why."

"But I have brought a gun with me."

"What a pity!" said the old man. "I can't let you stay here. You could kill me with your gun."

"So I must leave," said the boy.

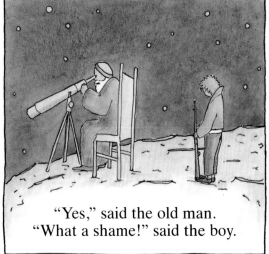

"Yes," said the old man. "What a shame!" said the boy.

"Are you sad?"
asked the old man.

"Yes," said the boy.
"I'd have liked to stay."

"Couldn't you throw away your gun?"

"Perhaps."

"And then you could stay here after all,"
said the old man.

"Perhaps,"
said the boy.

"And what would I do here?"

"You could
look through the telescope
and find out
why people are fighting down there."

"Why *do* they fight wars?"

"Because they don't know anything
about each other.

Because there are too many
people and they don't
realize the damage
they do.

Because some of them
starve, while others
have bread
on their tables.

Because they don't know
whether the iron
they forge
will be made into
spades or guns.

Because they are
too busy with their
own lives, to care
about anyone else.

If they could see what they're doing
to the world, they'd understand."

"But someone must show them!"
said the boy.

"Maybe,"
said the old man.
"But I'm too old
and too tired to do it."

Then the boy tossed away
his gun, and it fell through space
until it hit the planet
and broke into bits.

The boy stayed with the old man a long
time, forever looking through the
telescope, to try to understand
the people down below.

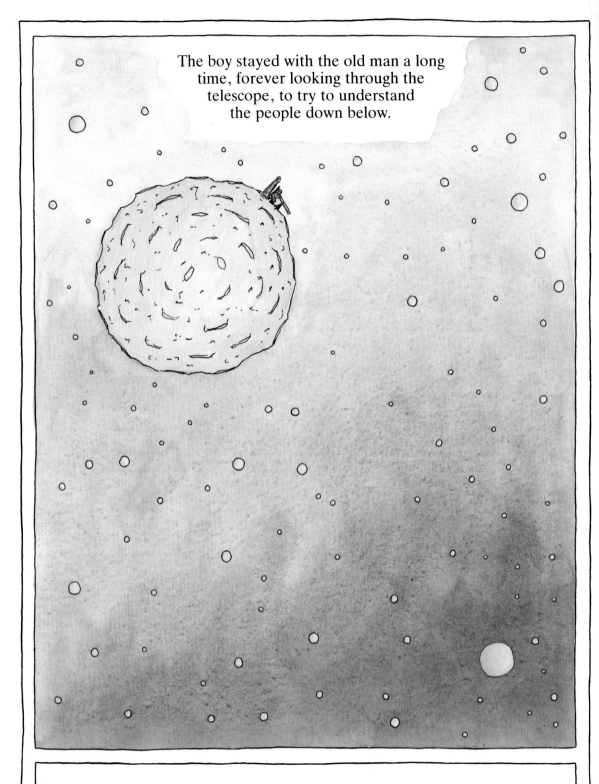

Who knows? Maybe he'll fly back one day
and tell his people everything he's learned.